ORANGE MAN BIG!

ORANGE I

COMICAL LEFT

CW00734756

Tarl Warwick
2023

ORANGE MAN BIG!

COPYRIGHT AND DISCLAIMER

FOREWORD

A hundred volumes of torrid lore could be concocted about the weird obsessions of leftists and Democratic Party partisans alike revolving around President Donald Trump. They are fixated on his genitals, his body mass index, his food choices, and every other aspect of his life. Some of them even have warped fantasies about his youngest son, involving cages and sadistic degeneracy.

It does not matter if "Big Don" is in office- even long after he is dead, I speculate that they will be writing creepy fan-fics about what they would like to do with his skeleton, analyzing how his decrepit corpse will look like in its casket, among other obsessive visualizations. This does not surprise me- hundreds of people owe their entire mediocre careers to finding new ways to rant about Trump; rants sometimes wildly veering off from conversation or debate, into the type of raving madness normally found only in the lunatic asylum.

These little stories follow a number of fictional protagonists through their bizarre, erotic meanderings- but while the protagonists do not exist, the basic premise is really more a tragi-comedy about the mental state of the obsessed left than a straight-up comedy- for it is rather sad that there are people in the world whose entire mental existence is completely reliant on what someone else has recently done or said. It's even more of a tragedy when you consider that some of these people make the majority of their income spouting off about the same single person- as though this wouldn't eventually lead to their entire paying career being defunct.

The psychological projection of the leftist is key here; constant fixations upon Donald Trump being a "loser", "ugly", "weak", etc, are just a form of mental masturbation in which their internalized feelings of worthlessness and weakness are externalized onto a foreign object or person, and then the weak individual begins hyperbolically fantasizing about how the *other* person must feel or be weak and helpless. If the other person scoffs at them, it is *invariably* taken by the weakling as evidence that the other person actually feels their *own* weakness. It is essentially a form of dissociative disorder, with some strange overlaps with multiple personality disorder- the leftist feels weak and so constructs an exterior self, of sorts, exhibiting their own feelings while being entirely autonomous. But in their own inability to reflect on their own weakness and internalized anger at themselves, they can only self reflect by first painting an image of themselves on something foreign. Rather amusing, no?

If you feel disgusted by some of the leftist fantasies related here, that is good! It is good to be disgusted by and averse to weakness and psychological decrepitude. If you find it amusing, that is also good; laughter is the best medicine and one all too often lacking in the lives of letists. Their sense of humor and irony is about as deficient as the protein intake of a vegan.

Sit back and enjoy some good ol' fashioned insanity because this humdinger ain't holding back.

ORANGE MAN BIG!

ALEXIS' STORY

Alexis was merrily strolling down the street of her upper middle class neighborhood one day, thinking happy thoughts about her Abuela and how her home repairs had been so graciously funded by a bunch of right wingers. She chuckled to herself jovially, thinking about how amusing it was to reject the money on her abuelas' behalf, and how she could skirt legality at a whim, for she was protected by the powers that be. The chuckling escalated to a wide grin and uproarious laughter that sounded like a chihuahua having its testicles twisted around in a vice as her enormous overbite jittered around, flashing in the sun, her tongue lolling about in her maw lasciviously.

"Today is a good day" she thought to herself, muttering it aloud, drawing the attention of passers-by; one man, thinking her a lunatic, crossed the street to avoid her, giving her a sideways glance as he shuffled off to get some avocado toast at the local hipster cafe.

On the edge of her shining, gated-community neighborhood there was a little section of the town which was not so pleasant. It appeased her bizarre fantasies to walk by its edge, simultaneously scoffing and looking down on the poor peasants there, while harboring illicit thoughts about how she could pay any of the assembled urchins and street bums there fifty dollars and they would run a train that would make her friend Pete giggle and blush.

Flipping her hair in a sassy manner, wiggling her big booty, Alexis did the shimmy-shake down the edge of the less fortunate neighborhood, drawing more attention, until she saw something in one of the decrepit, Malthusian alleys off the beaten path- one of many little hole-in-the-wall crevices lining the side street. She could make out a magnificent form in the back, a tall, well built fellow, with a rather familiar haircut. Curiosity was too much- she felt eager urges drawing her closer- hypnotically, slowly, making her way across the road, paying no heed to the honking of horns and cries of "get outta the way you stupid bitch!" elicited from drivers on the way to their meaningless middle class existences. She was better than they were, so she ignored their existence entirely.

Peering out from behind a pile of heroin needles, Alexis saw him; it was *really* him, the man of her fantasies, the man of the hour, the man with all the skills- Donald Trump himself.

She held her breath for what felt like ages, her face slowly morphing to a shade slightly shy of a beet when it has been overcooked, skinned, and sliced up into pieces before topping her twenty dollar arugula-kale salad. There he was- six foot three, and even grander than she ever hoped for. She caressed her breasts slowly, titillating herself through her outdated, hipster-ish mall girl top, when he turned to face her, looking right through the heroin pile into her very soul. Her breathing, which had returned, stopped altogether until she swooned, falling to the asphalt and regaining her composure, crawling like a subjugate to her sexual savior.

"Ah, hello" he said, adjusting his tie slightly, still surrounded by a small entourage of field agents dressed like they just walked off the set of Miami Vice, "I have been expecting you." He reached into his pocket, and Alexis was hoping he was fiddling with his peter, reciprocating her desire, but he was actually digging around for some food. "Dammit I know I have a spare here somewhere" he muttered, changing to his other pocket. "Aha! Behold." He pulled out a slightly mangled hamburger, like a priest withdrawing a communion wafer from the altar to feed a hungry supplicant the flesh of their god. "Come, it's time to put that mouth to use."

ORANGE MAN BIG!

Alexis was startled. She had not eaten meat for some time that didn't come from the local co-op. It was against her religion, and corporations were her enemy. But there, in his big, flawless hands, the hamburger looked mighty tasty. She wanted to feed from his hands like a pet pigeon, and so she crawled- yes, depraving her humanity she crawled like an animal across the heroin-needle strewn alleyway, mindful of the grins of the secret service agents as she made her way towards her savior. Leaning up, feet from her prize, she opened her mouth like Jaws when he flopped onto the deck of the Orca right before killing Quint, and upraised her mouth to the greasy, lukewarm meat.

"Psych!!!" Big Don pulled back the hamburger and began laughing, the field agents following suit. She had been tricked! The deprivation was too much, she could feel her insides squirm, her juices flow, her meat flaps swell with blood, pulsating obscenely. "Donald! Please!" She flipped over like an injured dog, arching her back and hissing, kicking her legs like a gazelle set upon by a pack of hyenas, spasmodically flailing her arms around, groaning and moaning and even peeing all over herself, a big wet blotch expanding down her legs, spraying through her tights wildly and dripping on the ground.

"I know what you think you want Alexis" Trump uttered, sternly, gravely, squinting his eyes into his deep, wizened furrows. "But I also know what you *really* want!"

With all her burning desire, she rose up like a wildcat, prowling around Big Don, panting and moaning, raising further to dance seductively- she wished she had a sari so she could culturally appropriate some of the dance moves she had learned when drunk and in college- he smiled slightly, dismissively, and simply stood in silence, watching her gyrate more and more frenetically, panting and working herself up, gasping, clawing at her clothes, thinking "why doesn't he want this steaming booty?"- more and more, minute by minute, until her legs- shaking with anticipation- simply gave out from under her, leaving her weeping and panting on the ground.

"You're a nasty woman" he said, looking down, taking a bite out of his hamburger and wiping some of the ketchup on his tie- which was red to begin with.

She looked up- how wise! At last, she knew; he really *did* know her darkest fantasies. Depraved, humiliated by her failure, writhing and gasping, she bent down and experienced the most fantastic, earth shattering orgasm she had ever had- leaving her sopping with more than just her own exhibitionist urine as she clutched her crotch with both hands, face to the side laying within sight of a half-hidden crack bag in among the garbage lining the alley. Indeed, the Donald knew her well- it was the subjugation, the masochism which was her *real* kink.

The agents began to filter out of the back as Trump slowly turned away, still periodically picking away at the edge of his hamburger, distracted momentarily by a couple of crackheads getting it on behind a dumpster to his side.

"I'll be back again next Thursday" he said, I hope you're ready to be a human toilet because It'll be cinco de mayo, and my people make the best taco bowls. Literally, everyone raves about them, simply the best, hands down, look at my hands, they're huge. And hand me that crack bag, I never touched the stuff, I think Hunter left it here. Bad man, really bad, so sad."

She never felt so loved in her life. After a lengthy recovery on the ground, she made her way back home. Her thoughts dwelt in paradise for days.

ORANGE MAN BIG!

JEFFREYS' STORY

Jeffrey busily sat by his computer, the glowing screen the only light he had seen in weeks- surrounded by cascading piles of empty bottles (some filled with urine- he hadn't had a drink in days because he lost track of which ones he had pissed in), mixed with empty and half empty, mold-caked pizza boxes and discarded cans of cheap beer. "You make your best internet posts when hammered" he quipped, laughing slightly at his own enlightened intellect.

Today, as most days, he was parked on the accounts of multiple people he branded as "far right"- he'd built a simple script that would make a sound when any of them posted. He usually got a quick nap in between his hot takes; today was a bit of a slow day, only fifteen self-aggrandizing posts, always including "holy shit" and "fuck"- he found that this added a level of sophistication to his replies and posts.

Donald Trump- his favorite figure of all- hadn't posted all day. It concerned him. So he made a new post; "Donald has been awfully quiet today... Fuckin shit! Maybe the dude finally died! Even his bastard family members wouldn't attend this losers funeral!" His audience applauded him reasonably for this historically important opinion; he sat up a little bit less hunched, swollen with pride at his enormous mental capabilities.

A little bell noise sounded on his computer. Someone he was stalking had posted... it was Trump himself! He had replied; "Oh yeah Jeff? Well, I'm in your hood. Pimps up hoes down, motherfucker, I'm five minutes away."

He was almost immediately enveloped in a sheen of greasy pizza sweat, aided by his chronic high blood pressure. His annoying hipster glasses slid down his nose and he pushed them back up, incapable of comprehending his win. Big Don himself had taken his bait. He hammered away at the keyboard like an orangutan attempting to coax a small animal out of a tree stump in order to crack its neck and play with the corpse. "Nobody is fooled Donny, you ain't a big boy. Even your own shit party hates you. Sad man!" He laughed again, deep in his wheezy, grease-soaked throat; the kind of laugh made by a ratty, greasy, pizza-faced punk that prides himself on his dad once owning a rat rod and rolling with some bad dudes.

A low, pounding thud sounded in the distance- the sound of a heavy, armored limo door being opened and closed. Despite his myopic aversion to sunlight he opened his blinds just a bit, peering out onto his neglected, weed-infested front lawn, squinting like a vampire into the glare, to see the man himself- Donald Trump, sauntering up the path to his home, flanked not by secret service, but by a pair of leather bound women carrying flails, barely able to walk in six inch heels.

"Oh fucking shit you gotta be kidding me" he said aloud, hefting his weak, anemic body up out of the gaming chair, sending it half spinning across the filthy room. Plowing through a barrier of pizza boxes and beer cans he finally opened his bedroom door and walked towards his front door. "Huh, I barely remember how the rest of my house looks... laughing out loud" he remarked, attempting to navigate the corridor- which was far less garbage-ridden but just as unkempt. His cat had died at some point in the last week, probably due to neglect and starvation, and he kicked its lifeless, maggot-swarmed body aside. A cloud of houseflies flew up from the decaying cadaver, forcing him to swat at them as he finally found his front door. It was jammed up from lack of use but he managed to force it open, staggering back as the morning sun topped the home next door, blinding him like the sun rising over the mountain blinded the uruk-hai in Lord of the Rings, roaring with myopic pain.

ORANGE MAN BIG!

"Well Jeffy, nice house!" Trump invited himself in, the dominatrixes entering shortly after, one picking up the dead cat and stuffing it in a leather bag for later- people were into some weird shit, after all.

He stood there, looking around- the dimly lit interior was grimy and the floor slick with a mix of dead cat drippings, urine, and pizza grease. "Haven't you ever hired a maid? I have. Wonderful things Jeffy, they clean and everything. I haven't cleaned anything in years. Some of them work cheap, Jeffy, I have a hundred of them, maybe more. Can't even keep track of the maids. I guarantee mine get the biggest Christmas bonuses, too."

Jeffy was starstruck. For years he had idolized this man and now, here he was, giving him advice on hiring house cleaners. "D-Donald? I didn't really mean..." His voice trailed off.

"Don't worry about it, said Big Don, sliding a finger along the grease-coated wall then wiping it off on the face of one of the dominatrixes. She moaned. "Ain't these gals something else? Reminds me of the eighties, I never did cocaine, I was too busy making millions of dollars. Great times. I met Ronald Reagan once."

Jeffy could feel himself getting turned on by the spectacular intelligence, the mere presence of Donald was making him horny- he found it comforting to be put in his place. But a flash of rage crossed his face. How dare this man belittle his home and his intellect!

"Donald, this isn't funny. I want that cock, holy shit!" He reached for Donalds large package but the dominatrixes grabbed him by both arms and held him fast. "Oh no Jeffy" he replied. "You couldn't afford the fee. I have a better idea. Sit him down."

The dominatrixes took out twine and bound his hands, his

ankles, and then strapped him to the moth-eaten chair in his front room. "Now, it's time for a *real* shitpost!"

Trump motioned to one of the dominatrixes, who proceeded to clean the neglected, poop-filled litterbox that sat beside the kitchen door. The smell of mold from the kitchen was even worse than the smell of week-old decaying cat turds. "I hope you're ready Jeffy, it's food time."

The dominatrixes set about preparing the cat shit-rehydrating it with warm water, popping it into a blender with some habenero hot sauce, and adding some of their own urine to the mix. They dangled their hanging labia perilously close to the blender blades as they pissed. Trump sat on the windowsill the entire time, remarking on the furniture. "That one is tacky" he said, jerking his thumb to point at the crappy, dollar store table by the front window. "But that over there, that's okay. Saw one in India once. Modi is a big fan of those." He gestured this time at some dishes lining the hallway as the dominatrixes re-entered the room.

"What this room needs is some fresh paint" he said, smirking at Jeffy, still chair bound.

They began rubbing the foul cat shit mixture on their bodies and proceeded to dance and smear themselves along the living room walls. The front site, the hallway entrance, all the way down the side; the one with the dead cat in her bag pulled chunks of its dried flesh and hair out and started smooshing them into the mix, sticking them to the shit-coated walls, laughing and referencing modern art.

"That's your kind of art Jeffy, not mine" she said, "I prefer fresher corpses." The crazy chick threw back her head and laughed until she almost choked.

ORANGE MAN BIG!

"Donald you're insane!" Jeffy said, but he was getting a little stiffy in his pants, and they all could see his small peter was trying to be a big boy. "No Jeffy, I'm an artiste, isn't that what you left wingers call them? I saw a modern art show once. Nothing good there. I threw out a pile of empty cans and someone tried to fine me ten thousand bucks, apparently it was some French guys display. Weird dude with a beret." Trump pulled out a piece of paper and scribbled on it. "Here, here's a check for ten thousand, you can buy some empty can French art or hire a maid. But my help comes at a price."

The dominatrixes approached him and his confusion turned to fear. Oh how they flailed their leather whips against him, driving the cat shit into his flesh! The burning lashes rained down on his thighs and chest, as they tattooed him with his own dead cats shit. "That'll teach you to fuck with me!" Trump yelled, clapping his hands and chanting "America will never fall to communist invasion!" Jeffy cried and screamed, but it was everything he wanted- except for Donald to be inside him with his mushroom. He pleaded through the pain for sex as the dominatrixes continued their sadistic whipping. "Oh no Jeffy, you people get off on not getting what you want. I'd be robbing you of the greater glory." The whipping ceased and, just as quickly as they arrived, the dominatrixes and Trump were gone. Trump gave him a wink as he closed the door behind him as Jeffy was wracked with multiple orgasms. Sitting there, bound to his chair, coated in cat excrement and his own sperm, he was finally happy. Thinking to the future, he decided he would make even more posts about Trump, hoping to eventually goad him into swinging by again.

LIL RONNYS STORY

The big night was finally upon them; Ronny had assembled a couple of hangers-on and was prepared to waltz down the red carpet, mingling with other rich and famous people, shaking their hands repeatedly, constantly fantasizing about urinating on his hands first, as a sort of joke.

The limo ride went smoothly- he remarked vacuously on the scenery- some gaudy lights here, a hotel with half darkened windows- one which was lit up displayed the silhouettes of what he could only interpret as a pair of men fisting one another in the ass. He chuckled, maybe he would do that later on. His entourage was entirely female though- his secretary and his fiance. "Oh well" he thought to himself, "everybody has a pooper."

When the limo stopped in front of the red carpet, waiting first for a few higher-list celebs, he flung the door open and, with a ponderous sigh, swung one caveman-like leg over the side and then the other, heaving his Neanderthal form out of the car and swaggering around a bit, raising his hands palm-up, staring at the flashing cameras, but then he saw something which disconcerted him- a broad shouldered but slightly hunched form, peering out from the edge of the crowd, clearly grinning at him. He advanced upon this visage, slowly, cocking his head to the side and looking upward slightly, like Vincent Price in one of his more theatrical moments.

"Yo... who are you, you smug muthafucka?"

The figure made no move, standing statuesque, like a Roman Praetorian Guard, hands dangling by his side.

"I said, who are you?"

ORANGE MAN BIG!

The figure stepped into the light as some of the gathered paparazzi fixated on the spectacle, hopeful that Ronny would go insane and they would have their thousand-dollar-a-print shot of the night to sell to the papers while felching themselves repeatedly like degenerates. It was him, the man himself, Big Don. Donald jutted his lower jaw out and furrowed his brow, in a mockery of Ronny. "Who you be?" He said in a monosyllabic monotone, "I make fire, me big man, ook ook." He laughed to himself, as did the gathered security guards.

"Oh you're in for it now, Donny Wonny. Did I ever show you my true powers?" Ronny dropped to the carpet, and immediately began shitting and pissing, filling his britches with foulness, rolling slowly from side to side and grabbing rump clumps to smear on his suit and his face. "Bet you didn't think of this one did you? You sad, stupid ape. I've been to one of your shitty hotels before, I made sure to shit in the garbage can before I left. Bet you feel real smart now lil' guy?" He continued to roll around but Trump was merely smirking, and this made Ronny angry.

"I think you missed a spot there. On your chin. I can still see some of your caveman wrinkles" Trump quipped, his smirk widening.

Ronny was flabbergasted- how dare Donny disrespect him? He had been hearing telepathic messages for years from Big Don, about how he wanted to have a sexual tryst with him involving chorizo and several jars of garden slugs. "Oh yeah? Well, then watch this!"

Ronny took a clump of his own pasty brown excrement and molded it into a ball, then proceeded to use his thumb to remove one of his eyeballs, shoving the ball of poo into the empty socket, moaning with pain, expecting his love interest to be impressed. "Lookit me Donny!" he cried, in fervor, "I'm giving you the stink eye! Get it? You wacky nutjob."

The paparazzi was now flashing its cameras so quickly that several veterans in the back row had flashbacks and had to leave the red carpet. A thousand bystanders had their smartphones out and were recording the incident- the live streams alone were beginning to overrun the legacy media broadcasts of the resplendent show, racking up millions and millions of viewers, crashing several smaller websites altogether.

"And now the coup de grace, Donny!" He pulled down his pants and painfully began forcing his index finger into his urethra. "My power... is... unlimited!" He gasped between words, crippled with insanity and pain. "I own you!... You mother... fucker..."

Ronny collapsed to the red carpet, spasming with delight. Donald produced a paper from his pocket, proffering it to Ronnys fiance. "I think it's time to sign the papers, if you know what I mean" he said, and she scribbled her signature onto the paper as several men in white lab coats emerged from behind Trump, hoisting the now gibbering, incoherent Ronny into an ambulance. "Now my job is done" Don concluded, receding like a ninja back into the crowd.

Ronny, delusional and insane, nonetheless realized what Donald had done for him. As the ambulance made its way to the lunatic asylum, he now realized he was free to live his life the way he always wanted to- smearing his excrement on himself and others and making a fool of himself in a masochistic, self-deprecating manner.

ORANGE MAN BIG!

NONCY STORY

It was another boring summer day in congress. The sweaty humidity was making the boozy scents wafting off every surface even thicker- the smell of splashed wine, ale, liquor, every possible alcohol ever manufactured, built up in the floor boards, wallpaper, furniture, for two centuries without cease.

Noncy sipped a bit of champagne- not the champagne those dumb peasants drank- the good stuff, a couple hundred a bottle. The bubbles made her head swim, and she giggled, clutching her sagging, elderly flesh, wiggling her arms around and cackling as the dangling skin folds wubbered back and forth like the wrinkled, fatty flesh of a pig or a walrus.

Her office door suddenly swung open with a bit of creaking, like her elderly joints, reminding her of her advanced age, and there he was- the man for the hour- Donald Trump.

She protested, "Get the hell out of here, you oaf!" But inside of her mind there were naughty thoughts racing, her pulse quickening, threatening to cause her ancient vascular system to pop off and give her a stroke. "I don't want you in my office!"

She pretended to call security but was curious why he was there as Big Don trundled across the room, appearing to inspect his surroundings. "I like the décor here, look at that lamp. Nice, shiny, not too much not too little. I have dozens of lamps at the Mar a Lago like this. Fantastic things. You can read at night a lot easier when you own lamps."

He turned halfway, peering down instead of at Noncy. "I just came to use the restroom. Ronny ruined the one downstairs. I'll be a minute. Do you mind?" His question was really just a statement and he entered the private bathroom, closing the door behind him, sitting down and relieving himself noisily, mumbling sporadically about what he had eaten, the bathroom fixtures, and the President of France and his own bathroom decorations. He flushed, but the toilet backed up from his presidential poop load, and it almost flooded to the floor.

"Well I guess lunch is a dish best served lukewarm" he said, winking and exiting the office.

Noncy was flabbergasted. This oaf just clogged her toilet. Like a strong empowered member of congress she sighed and went into the potty, the stench overpowering her and making her wretch, but she swallowed down her own booze-puke so as not to lose any of the alcohol in her half-full belly. She had to be less than sober if she was going to deal with her next couple of meetings; first she had a meet and greet with a bunch of badly behaved grade schoolers, and then she had to go hold a meeting with the progressives. She didn't know which group was more puerile and stupid.

She managed to work the plunger into the bowl, and smooshed it up and down into the magnificent plopping honker, trying to shove that shit down the toilet drain, but it just wouldn't budge. Congressional commodes were just not built to handle executive excrement. So she reached in and began scooping out the foul pasty remains by hand.

While it was nasty, and smelly, she started to get aroused at the thought of holding the turd of such a powerful figure. She marveled at the slightly wrinkled exterior of the giant poo- little crenelated bits, studded with some corn and gritty grainy bits. Clearly Trump had been gorging on his taco bowls again. She wondered if he had one of Jeb Bushes "guaco bowles" there as a joke. She had one on her desk, just to remind her colleagues of who the boss was- it sure wasn't Jeb.

She smooshed a little bit of the poo up between her legs onto her own ass. It felt warm, like Donald was hugging her anus. She felt that he cared for her, telepathically, in a moment of delusion caused by excessive decades-long alcoholism.

And in that moment she wanted to make herself filthy. To deprave herself in a show of masochistic obeisance. *Just this once* she thought to herself, *just once, I'll let myself go.*

She began picking little corny bits out of the presidential expulsion, sticking them to her foul skin, pulling off her clothes and working smears of brown into the wrinkled folds of her elderly, saggy flesh. Cackling with delight, she began pooping uncontrollably, mixing the slimy alcohol shits in with the pasty presidential poo pile and began making a few crap statues on the floor, whispering to herself in insanity, pretending they were speaking with one another.

But she had a meeting to go to. She got her clothes back on, washed her hands a bit, and proceeded to go meet with the grade schoolers, leaving her crap statue puppet show for later that evening- she'd be pulling an all nighter, but thankfully she had about five more booze bottles under her desk; "so" she said aloud as she made her way to the meeting room, "it's all good."

All the children and teachers alike, assembled there, screwed up their faces when they smelled the poop-coated wretch arrive, but she did not notice- she was on cloud nine from the mighty gift she had been given, and she just assumed they were all just being regular, normal, stupid children making faces.

ORANGE MAN BIG!

MIKEY STORY

The day had started out well for Mikey. It was one of those rare times when his wife would not be physically with him, so he had taken some chemical castration pills, locked his mere twanger inside his diamond-studded chastity belt (this was masculine, in his mind- the diamonds were mined by slaves and it made him feel like a big Kahuna), and locked the front door double. His back door was always locked, and he frequently told this to guests, while chuckling to himself. The feeling of the cold metal chastity belt gave him goosebumps. It felt good to be a bitch who knew his place. He wished his wife were there to spank him, to tilt her head up in a better-than-you way, looking down at his tiny wee wee and laughing at his pathetic subjugation. That would really make the day even brighter.

With his sinful nature suppressed, he busied himself puttering around in his living room, enjoying the feeling of his low-slung, mottled, wrinkly balls wiggling back and forth below the skeletal cage enclosing his "man"hood. He put on some good coffee and extracted a sleeve of pictures from his wallet- gazing at them; pictures of mutilated bodies in a foreign war somewhere. He could feel his throbbing member strain against its cage impotently and he clasped his legs together like a kid trying to hold their pee in while waiting for the bathroom stall to be unoccupied. It was sheer bliss- the desire, the suppression, the physical enslavement.

He heard a strange noise from the back of the house, and his oversized, chimpanzee-like ears perked up. Someone was inside of the house! And they had sinned by coming in the back door! He peered around the corner at the end of the kitchen, and could see nothing down the hallway- lined with several doors, which were closed. A slightly wonky deers' head- an example of bad taxidermy- leered down halfway through the hall, reminding him that he needed to pretend to be a redneck gun lover soon to try and drum up some more book sales, or his wife would humiliate him again and not for sexual reasons.

Slowly he crept down the hall, mindful that it could be one of Pauls' lovers with a hammer waiting there to bean him in the head and violate his sin-hole. He had only had his sin-hole violated once before, by a priest, when he was a college student. Oh how it had burned his young rectum! And the priest had not even given him a reach-around.

But it was no burglar or psychotic Democrat party stalker- no, the figure was standing at the side of the room, admiring the door he had just walked through.

"Nice door. Wasn't locked up though. I always lock my doors. Anyone can come in through an unlocked door. In Britain doors cost more money. What is it they use? Pounds and Pence I think- they left the European Union. Great guy that Nigel fellow."

He winked at Mikey as he ran his hands up and down the back door, smirking with an obvious insinuation. "You know Mikey you really violated my trust before. Maybe it's time you violate yourself, you know?"

Mikey was beside himself. After all, his wife wouldn't know, would she? He was throbbing like the dying heart of a Falun Gong dissident before having their organs harvested by communists and then sold to the Cheney family. "Donald I... I'm, sorry for..."

Trump cut him off. "Fuggetaboudit, as my Italian voters say. Great food, weird family structure. I loved my mother but she could be overbearing. Never understood it. Spaghetti is a great meal. Trump Tower sells the best spaghetti. We hired an Italian chef to make it. Name's Luciello or something. I call him Pavarotti."

21

ORANGE MAN BIG!

The throbbing just got harder with every dripping, sexy syllable Big Don uttered. Mikey could feel his sweaty dong slipping out of its cage. "I can't do this!" He ran back down the hallway, genuflecting and punching himself, trying to get the sinful homosexual thoughts out of his head.

But the thoughts were too much. Mikey began orgasming even though he was clasped tightly inside his peepee-cage. Trump was dancing around in the back room laughing and tossing dishes around, smashing them. "Just think of these as drone strike explosions, Mikey, that oughtta do the trick!" He laughed and yelled. Mikey spasmed on the floor, mindful of his sin, mindful of his subjugation, and failure.

"I don't want to see another man naked. All the girls like me. Try buying one of them a Ferrari sometime. A really good one, you would never believe it. Unbelievable." Trump had his back turned and, without uttering another word, left the house, closing the back door. A slight click let Mikey know that while he had violated himself and sinned against Jesus Christ, his back door was, now, at last, locked up again, preventing him from being assured Hellfire.

"Oh Donald..." He wept, grasping his sticky member as he laid on the floor, decorated with a badly outdated carpet from the Kennedy era. "Oh... you big, big man. Oh my lord Jesus... I am sorry." He cradled his head in his hands, and wept for hours, both in joy for the bliss he had experienced, and pain and sorrow for his lack of self discipline and his ingrained sexual weaknesses. He spent the subsequent hour scrubbing his entire body from top to bottom with a wool sponge in the shower until his cuticles and the webbing between his hands and feet bled freely. At last he was suffering as Jesus suffered. This was a great gift. He couldn't wait until his wife and dominatrix returned, to show her his newfound power.

LIZZY STORY

Lizzy had been unemployed for some time. There were various ads for work that was available but most of it was beneath her stature as a former member of congress. Hocking cheap merchandise on television? That was a hard pass. Six figures to shill for a mere major colonel working with the CIA? There was hardly anything even deserving of a second glance.

But then she saw *the* ad, writ large- she'd have to relocate to Florida to fill it but it seemed decent; a high six figure salary, promising to work with the former president. She got a little wet and squirmed in her ergonomic office chair just thinking about it; she despised Donald Trump, and now was her time to shine; what scandalous paperwork and digital intrigue there must be at the Mar a Lago? Getting paid to undermine democracy was her forte, and now her self aggrandized wit would truly be of good use.

Using her CIA connections she managed to quickly whip up a fake identity, hoping to bamboozle the old scoundrel. And bamboozle she did- or so she thought. Her pig-like voice wubbered with chortling glee as she was ushered in on her first day, having set up a nice rental home less than a half mile away. The décor was not her style- rather traditional- she preferred postmodernism, although she had needed to pretend that moose antlers and exposed wood was her bag back when the rubes in the west had hired her dumb ass.

"My name is Joan Pastinak" she announced, when queried by the secret service and the on-site private security force. She squinted, hoglike, as she waited for them to examine her credentials at the security checkpoint, glaring at them, daring them to question her authority. The guns on their waists were making her hotter than her secret crush, Tulsi, doing pinup shots next to an active volcano and she had some difficulty standing. The guards assumed she was just drunk like everyone else ever associated with politics seemed to be in times of import, and waved her in, accepting the dubious documents.

The first two weeks were unremarkable. She had to keep a low profile, while simultaneously filing paperwork, milling about randomly, and enjoying her evenings waddling around in the Jacuzzi in a porcine manner. Having established some camaraderie with a few other workers, and covered for by a few planted insiders, she commenced thereupon with her plan.

Accessing paperwork was easy, so she began photographing everything she could, offloading the documents in real time to her lucrative handler. Oh what accolades she would gain! Finally, the Teflon Don would be put down like a diseased orangutan. But as she continued processing the paperwork, she felt a sense of unease- which turned to panic as a hulking, broad-shouldered shadow emerged from the hall and loomed over her like a stony monolith.

"Hello Lizzy. Nice phone. Not made in China. See, when you make a lot of money, you can buy things that will still work in a year. I do a lot of business with China, but I still think we need to protect our trade and currency. You can say whatever you want about Chinese trade disparities but they have some real cut-throats managing things, not like the pathetic people here." He gazed down a full foot at her stout stature, his jaw set, squinting slightly. "Hey, I have a better phone though. Try this one."

Lizzy took the phone from Big Don, hands shaking- she feared she had been observed in her operations. The casing was clearly gold, etched with an image of Trump himself. "Hey Lizzy, tell you what, sit there in the chair with this phone in your lap and I'll use your phone to call you. I'm what you might call a phone man. I understand phones like nobody. The phone you're holding made every one of my yuge tweets by the way."

ORANGE MAN BIG!

The thought enthralled her and she obeyed, sitting obligingly in the office chair, the gold cased phone between her legs, waiting for her sexual salvation.

He called her number- which of course was tied to her resume. The vibrator on the phone was as powerful as Big Dons sultry voice in one of his more demure moments. The spasm of the phone rubbed her in just the right way as she suppressed a moan, oozing fluid as she squirmed.

"D-donald... I" she stammered "The paperwork... The chair..."

"I don't care if the chair gets wet" he replied, waving her off. "The phone will keep vibrating until the battery dies or you end the call so, try not to get distracted with your paperwork or you're fired." He wandered back off, taking her phone with her and posting bizarre tweets as she turned back to her scanning work. Obediently, she continued to scan the documents and send them to her handler, having been commanded by her master to do so- she cried with joy as her legs shook, and with sadness; for she had betrayed the one, massive, powerful man who could truly ever make her happy. But she was not fired. The paperwork she was scanning over was nothing more than thousands of pages documenting delivery orders to the mansion involving food from a hundred local restaurants. Reading them got her off even more; Donald really did like his hamburgers, as any masculine man does, and there was not a hint of soy or kale smoothie anywhere. She eventually passed out, the phone slowly dying, and she awoke to a happy, sunny Florida morning, her own phone silently replaced on her lap where Big Dons had been. For her, phone sex was the best sex she could hope for, and she had to hurry off to her room to change her pants before her next work shift.

ORANGE MAN BIG!

DASHY STORY

He was eighteen going on eighty. His baby face, still wet behind the ears, layered with wrinkles and lines from collagen loss due to a steady diet of soy, kale shakes, and roasted insects. He usually bought them directly from Schwab- good ol' Santa Klaus didn't even give him a markup because he was so good at making astroturfed, pedestrian takes on the internet. The screen glare from his several digital devices were prematurely aging his skin too, all messed up and mottled, his overly large, oogly eyes staring into the digital void for ten hours a day. He hadn't gotten a full nights' rest in weeks, since he set his phone to notify him every time someone posted something he found objectionable- and that was a long list of subtopics.

He spent his off time stuffing dead cricket bits in his urethra, then pissing them out against a target he had erected against the wall of his dimly lit basement lair- a lair replete with shelf after shelf of funko pops and other materialistic trash made using petroleum products. Like a true goofy, he felt this made him "hip" and "progressive"- but today he had bigger things to do, groaning as he had to expose himself to the tyranny of the sun outside, grabbing his half-clean suit and throwing it on in order to show his resplendence to the world which did not deserve his very existence.

An SUV took him to the big affair- a shiny, jet black SUV which averaged fifteen miles to every gallon of gasoline it was filled with, its inefficient, guzzling tank exposed on the underside to let the peasants know he was their gated-community-dwelling economic superior. Like a microcosmic Al Gore, he gazed out the tinted window at the proles outside, no doubt gathered to view him just for a moment, as the vehicle coasted into a hotel parking area, so that he would not have to walk too far before making it back indoors, where he was safe. He watched the SUV depart with his watery, sad-sack eyes and then entered the hotel rotunda, being greeted by a couple of staffers with problem glasses and red hair- his kind of gal, if he was into gals.

But he had a dark secret, and it made his drippy wee-wee palpitate with delight when he thought of it. What he really wanted was to furtively eat the turds of Donald Trump.

He sighed despite himself as the problem-glasses squad led him to yet another predictably boring room full of people with more social clout than he had. Sighing, that is, until he was led by the bathrooms off the side of the main hall, which adjoined an unfortunately well-lit convention center.

The roar of a toilet distracted him- then he was distracted from the roar by the presence of several guards in black suits wearing ear pieces and aviators and handguns. Oh how he hated handguns. They were tools of the devil. His indignance rose for a moment and his wrinkled face turned a redder shade of pale, until the man himself- Big Don- swaggered out of the mens' room, looking manly indeed, his shoulders as broad as a propaganda statue of Stalin. The stench of Cinco de Mayo taco bowls wafted out from the door, which Donald held open, grinning.

"Dashy, you give me so much attention on the internet" he said, looking down and nodding slightly, "I rarely give people attention, it gives them weird ideas, like that one Russian magnate I met with years ago, name was Molotov something-or-other, strange guy, had terrible interior decorators, everything was blue- even his carpet. I never liked blue carpets."

Dashy dashed through the door, all but ignoring Big Don, who turned to watch as a frantic search of the toilet stalls began. There were five of them, all in a row. A couple of them didn't even have a lining of petulant graffiti scrawled on the doors- this, after all, was a posh bathroom. In the fourth stall, he found his prize-

ORANGE MAN BIG!

Big Dons big shit had not completely flushed, as he had briefly feared, but that seasoned ground beef, cheesy goodness, all of that guacamole... the first flush had barely even cleared the water, leaving a hefty hoagie behind for Dashy to glue himself to like a starving housefly.

He shoved his whole head in the bowl, briefly smelling the scent of Donald Trumps ass cheeks squelched formerly against the bowl itself, his greasy, prematurely balding hair spread out like a veil as if to hide his shame and sin as he pushed his whole face into the pasty shit log, caking himself with foulness in a strange imitation of a minstrel show. It was bliss- absolute bliss, his masochistic desire for a real mans' poop to humiliate and defile him.

Trump said something from the doorway but Dashy didn't hear it, his ears were caked with poop and he forced his sallow, wrinkly face deeper into the bowl, savoring every molecule of Donalds feces as he licked and titillated his tongue with the foulness, retching but forcing himself to keep it down, like a good and obeisant servant, utterly subjugated, totally owned by his superior. Now he knew what wagies felt like when they were berated by their night shift manager- it was all he ever wanted, all he ever needed; he lifted the squishy remnant of Donalds into his arms, and he didn't want to speak at all, for words were not necessary, and would only dampen this holy moment.

Donald was still there, watching as his taco-baby was cradled lovingly, and with a wink, he withdrew, half-jogging down the hallway, out to his limo, having given another satisfied customer what they wanted. Dashy knelt on the floor, kissing his shit baby, promising to take it home and finally mature enough to raise his "child."

CENKY STORY

Obesity was a big problem. DNC funding had dried up and Cenky hadn't been able to replace his office chair in a good month- it was beginning to creak under the strain of his bulk, and reek with thousands of farts, staining the black leather with a strange sheen, leaving an uncleanable mess behind which caused the night janitor to gag. A steady diet of buffalo chicken wings, soda pop, and nacho fries was taking its toll on his intestines. He lifted a ponderous ass cheek and let loose a rectal belch, practically shitting in frustration as he hate-watched Donald Trumps latest video release. The crazy man was now pledging to crack down on the fentanyl trade; where would Cenkys fan base acquire their communist-friendly drugs from? They'd have to start getting it from trailer skinheads, thus funding more racism. That just wouldn't do.

His beady, untrustworthy eyes squinted as he glared at the screen, silent, brooding, his flabby jowls mere inches from the pixels before he started tossing papers randomly around his desk, yelling about bigotry, stuffing a handful of post-it notes into his mouth and chewing on them, bellowing in rage through his self imposed muzzle. Silencing himself was orgasmic, and he grabbed at his mere twanger with one crude, greasy hand, smearing nacho sauce all over his crotch.

Back in the day his office had been a go-to place but now it looked a little bit dungeonesque- a few of the lights were fizzling out, and the hallway outside was no longer a bustle of activity. He was a fat, shallow-minded has-been, and he knew it. So he projected his sense of insecurity and impotence off on the smug orange man on his screen.

"NOOOOO you fat, mushroom-cock oaf!" He spat out the post it notes all over the room in a show of manliness, wiping cheese and beer foam on his screen, shorting it out. The image faded, fizzled, the pixels all messed up as he smeared his filth across the electronics, then heaving his enormous body up on the table, in a foul semblance of the beaching of a whale. His obscene, tiny penis stood out of his ill-fitted trousers as he dragged himself forward, making incoherent noises, gazing in madness at several pictures of Donald Trump which he had mounted on his wall; "they are more useful than orange man" he had thought when posting them there- and to him, they were, he could just glance at them and start off on an angry rant effortlessly.

The congealing nacho cheese clogging his arteries finally took their toll and he clutched his chest through his cheap suit, angina setting in. It scorched his heart like fire- oh what bliss! The sheer masochistic agony. He ejaculated on the computer, frying it entirely- that would set him back a bit, it was purchased back when his show was solvent and not constantly downsizing. Orange man had done it again- even at a distance- his sheer indignance and anger at Trump simply *existing* had done the trick. Exhausted, his heart still palpitating, Cenky collapsed across the desk, kicking the screen across the room and sprawling out on the floor, punching himself in the chest and bellowing like a starving wildebeest, until his chest returned to normal, gasping on the floor, filling his trousers with a fetid slop which resembled sloppy joe sauce as he fell asleep, dreams of Donald paddling his rump with an electric flyswatter making him sleep sweet and sound in his deep seated madness.

ORANGE MAN BIG!

JOE STORY

Joe busied himself at the little desk in the oval office; he had the mind of a first grader- which was fortunate since that was also his preferred age range on dates. He fiddled around with a few colorful blocks, babbling to himself and drooling a bit- he had bran muffin crumbs stuck to his suit, and his tummy was rumbling from his brunch and his prune smoothie. He couldn't wait to do a doo-doo stinky ca-ca later and have a secret service agent change his adult diaper.

He pulled out some photographs from his lil' desk and almost went wee-wee; someone had replaced his pictures of dead, blistered bodies in Afghanistan and Yemen with pictures of the man himself; his nemesis and superior, Big Donald Trump.

"Orange man bad!" He stuck a thumb in his mouth to self-soothe, but it didn't work. "Angry!" He shouted, jogging out of the room and into the hall like a deranged chimpanzee on a banana binge. He pretended he was chasing his dog to grab its tail, as he managed to jog past the handlers in the hallway who had orders to keep him there until his naptime. He would lose big boy points for this one, that was for sure, but as he squinted his eyes like the inbred kid in Deliverance, he determined that he was really going to haul off this time. HE was the big boy in the oval office now, by golly, and he was gonna prove it!

Joe stripped his suit off as he jogged through- at least his legs still worked, more or less. A handler tried to grab him but he managed to shove him away and the poor lad toppled over a table- he didn't want to be the one who had to tackle someone who might suffer a hip fracture from it, so he halfassed his grab.

His adult diaper was bulging out of his pants, as the handler tugged them down from behind while half-spinning across

31

the table- and Joe laughed at him in an infantile manner. His doo doo undies were showing! But there was no doo-doo in them yet- that would have to wait until he ingested some fiber later.

"Hahaha! Old Joe ain't so weak after all you little scalawag!" He chuckled as he dashed out the door, intent on scoping out the property for Donald or his henchmen. In his alzheimers delusions he imagined that he was actually a superhero- a great leader who would finally kick the orange orangutans ass and get his war death pictures back. Then, America would be safe another day.

Donald was watching from outside the fence, with a few MAGA-hat wearing staffers and a small crowd, which assembled to see Biden evade a second handler, who tripped in her haste on the steps and went head over heels into the shrubbery, and Biden bent down, grimacing, sniffing her hair. He smelled more booze than shampoo. "Too old" he thought to himself, pushing her face into the shrubs as he bent back up and scoped out the fenceline. There he was- the old villain! There was Donald!

He jogged over, hollering random threats, and Donald stood there laughing, but then Joe bent down in the treeline- he had a secret arsenal he had been saving there, in a little box, for just such an eventuality. The box was full of dog shit. He grabbed up a clump of foul, fossilized dog crap and tossed it at the fence, where it impacted on the rail, releasing a dusty blast of dry, mummified poo on some of the onlookers. He had missed his target, but managed to foul some henchmen, so that was progress indeed. No malarkey.

"Joe, I think you missed your nap. I have your pictures, here, take em'. I never take naps, I sleep about five hours a night. Sometimes it's the soda Joe, it has caffeine in it. Wonderful thing- only drug I ever tried. Sometimes I just want to get more work in."

ORANGE MAN BIG!

Joe approached the fence, staring squintingly into the face of his nemesis. "You apologize to me?" He asked, hunched down slightly- his arthritis was acting up from all the physical activity.

"Yes Joe." He handed over the pictures of charred corpses. "Jill wants to see you back inside I think. Good wife. Not as hot as Melania, but what the hell, right? I sold steaks once."

Joe fondled the pictures lovingly, remembering each drone strike he had watched live as miserable, meaningless lives had been ended by his iron fisted order. A handler managed to get him by the arm and lead him back inside the White House, and he was tucked into his little nappy, so he could get his nice warm bran muffin and a shot of prune juice to have his afternoon bowel movement. The warmth of his cozy little baby bed was matched only by the warmth of his thoughts as he replayed, over and over, mentally, the fantastic tale of how he had finally bested orange man, that big mean neanderthal, and how powerful and tough he was. His thoughts slowly melted into a dementia haze and became more and more scattered as he drifted off to sleep, his wife watching over him, next to several very nervous handlers who knew she would berate them and throw plates at their heads for failing to corral her husband.

ORANGE MAN BIG!

HILLY STORY

Hilly stood staring into the mirror, fully nude, her mottled, discolored skin sagging off her withering body, cadaveresque and foul, breasts dangling pendulously. She had a little bit of shit stuck in the monumental wrinkles on her ass- it was hard to wipe the poo stains off and sometimes took ten minutes; but a strong, empowered woman like her had no time for such tomfoolery, and if others were subjected to the faint scent of her poop, it didn't bother her; it was fun to think of inconveniencing others.

Next to the mirror was a little picture of Donald Trump, signed on the back; a little "gift" from the long past. He was there grinning in a cut-throat businessman-like manner, and it really turned her on. Something about his smug "I am better than you" face just really did the trick. She cackled to herself slightly, for she knew she was actually better than he was. For a few minutes, thinking of this, she practiced her sardonic grin in the mirror- elocution, after all, was important, but she had a brunch to make, so she reluctantly abandoned the Trump picture and the bathroom, throwing on a robe and descending to the kitchen. Other than her, the house was empty- Bill was off cavorting and her daughter was busy sealing a business deal up in China; what a wondrous and splendid time, having the house to yourself!

With nobody around to judge her, she could enjoy brunch the way she truly wanted- by stuffing all the ingredients in various orifices before cooking it. Her clown car was ponderous and made for an excellent way to warm up food, so in went a banana, while a couple of hardboiled eggs were stuffed under her sagging milk jugs. The actual milk was racist, so she opted for orange juice, sipping it while her meal got nice and warm and comfortable in her skin folds.

A knock at the door distracted her; a knock at the door at

such an hour usually meant some ignoramus from the third world wanted to kiss ring and get some money, or perhaps a crate of rocket launchers to go ethnically cleanse some dissident population. Work was work, after all, and lucrative, so she didn't mind waiting for her eggs and banana. She intended to smear both of them on some toast. She shuffled to the door, but there was nobody there- down at her feet, though, was a little basket, with an envelope attached. She retrieved it, looked around, saw nobody, shrugged, and headed back inside- her bottom was briefly visible to the outside world as her robe swished when she turned and closed the door behind her behind.

The note inside of the envelope simply read, "from a friend" and had a little winking emoji on the end. It looked an awful lot like a tweet, and the hair stood on end on her neck and back- could it be? Did *he* really just gift her something tasty?

Inside the basket was a little cardboard box containing a gigantic breakfast taco. A little picture of Jill Biden was stapled to the side of the box as well- an obvious inside joke. It was a Trump taco bowl! Donald had indeed gifted her a meal- and it was a prototype! She quickly dialed the man himself on the phone. It went to voicemail, but the recording was just as fantastic:

"Hey, it's Donald here. I'm not at the phone right now. Enjoy your breakfast. Yes, it's the very first one. We decided to branch out into more kinds of tacos. We even got our own guaca-bowle- it's pretty nice. Only 29.99 at any of our locations. I guarantee you'll love the new breakfast bowl taco; made with quail eggs, the best freshest Wisconsin cheese, and plenty of sauce. The sauce makes the taco. You have to have good sauce. My competitors sauces are bullshit. Bye."

After the beep she left a brief message thanking Donald for breakfast. The banana she squeezed out of her stench trench onto the floor, although she saved the eggs for later- maybe she'd devil them. She enjoyed the idea.

The breakfast taco bowl was delicious. The sauce was, as Donald had predicted, just about perfect. She didn't even need to grab hot sauce from her handbag, and the flavor really made *her* sauces flow too. She quickly loaded a video of Donald deriding her on the internet, and reached into her robe, rubbing a little bit of cheese and sauce on her crevasse as she continued slowly to eat, savoring every bit of the taco. She took a piece of the hard, crusty shell, and scooped up some of her sauce-mixed love juice and ate it; just the smell made her writhe in ecstasy.

Truly, the man had delivered. The taco sauce being rather spicy made her tummy rumble, so she had to half-jog to the bathroom to unleash a liberal log into the latrine, and the foulness caked her wrinkly ass region anew. What a fine morning.

ORANGE MAN BIG!

KATHY STORY

It was a blustery, dark night; the crackling fire did little to warm Kathys cold, dead heart as she sat by the pale glow of her computer screen, face taut in botox-enhanced concern as she took a stroll through the internet, deliberately finding things that would vex her, so she could complain. Her career in comedy was now, itself, a joke, and it had been a few years since she was remotely culturally relevant, and this displeased her.

"How will I manage to buy my fine wine if I can't find a way to make money?" She muttered to herself, "I'll have to switch to box wine, like a peasant!"

A faint tap-tap-tapping sounded around the side of her Mcmansion. It made its way across the wall, across one window, across more wall, and towards the side door, which normally looked out over a lakeside vista- but the sky was black and the wind full of leaves and rain and fog- she had to turn her entire body to the side, squinting as she peered in that direction- the botox had her neck skin so tight she couldn't turn it more than thirty degrees or so without pain.

"Who the fuck is there?" She shouted, pounding her withered, anemic fists against the arm rests of her lounge chair, muttering to herself in an elderly fashion as she rose up, joints aching because of the bad weather.

The clattering continued- the tap tap tapping rose slowly up the side of the wall, now plinking and plunking along the edge of the roof. She could hear someone struggling to get up further, then footsteps up the incline, stopping momentarily.

"Ho ho ho!" The deep sound echoed down her chimney and a puff of soot came down, flaring up the fire, and then a blast of extinguishing powder came roaring down, scattering half-dead embers across the slate tiles, ash wafting up into the air and making her cough and gag. She puked a little bit of wine into her throat, but swallowed it back down- waste not want not.

The fire was entirely dead, and a tall man in a red suit came down, stomping the ashes before he crouched into the room, bending low under the overhanging mantle. It wasn't Santa though- it was someone far more magical, and all the gas she had been retaining in her bowels came poofing out in a dry, continuous stream, like the spores of a puff mushroom squeezed by a grade schooler.

"Nasty weather. Nice fireplace. Don't worry, we'll stoke this up again quick." Big Don turned, placed a sack on the ground next to the tiles, then tossed a few logs into the fire and lit it with a hip flask full of kerosene. "It's like a, what do they call it, Vladimir cocktail or something. Seen 'em before, these days they use wind-proof matches to light them." He chuckled at his joke and the fire roared up, cheerfully crackling. "Now" he said, "I have some gifts for you. Poor girl. I know you like modern art. I prefer older art. Have dozens of pieces at the Mar a Lago actually. Tried to rent the Mona Lisa, those French drive a hard bargain."

He produced a canvas from the sack. It smelled like shit. "I smeared some dog shit on this. It's my very first art piece. I call it 'your career' Kathy. It might smell bad but I signed it, here, you see my signature."

He had indeed signed the canvas. The dog shit had the form of an enormous smiley face, with some random scribbling around the sides. "Don't worry, I declassified it so you don't have to worry about getting raided by the FBI" he quipped, chuckling again at his humor, looking like he had just ingested some of her wine.

"Donald, thank you, you piece of shit." She was simultaneously aroused by the presence of such an intimidating man, and yet indignant and angered. "I have to... get back to work."

"Work? I work harder than anyone. People used to call me the worker, because I sleep four hours a night. Never understood sleeping in. Can't get rich being sleepy. I called Joe sleepy a few times. Oh, here's another gift. Merry whatever it is today." He wiped ash from his red suit and produced a bag from the sack, presenting it to her. Inside was a decapitated head.

"This one is real, Kathy, it's the head of a terrorist. We blew him up back when I was the one overseeing the situation in Syria. Had the head preserved in honey. We only use real honey at the Mar a Lago. Goodnight, Kathy." He exited the home by the front door, tracking ash everywhere, randomly tossing a bottle of cleaner and some paper towels by the door, leaving without a further word. The decapitated head- a symbol of Trumps power, and also of her career- it was magnificent. She licked the sheen of honey caking the dead flesh, and it was awfully good. Cackling, she scraped some of the death honey off the head and added it to her wine glass, refilling it liberally. Thanks to the generosity of Donald, it'd be a good night. She closed her browsers full of rage bait and immediately went to her favorite pornographic website. It wasn't just the storm outside that was going to be wild that night...

ORANGE MAN BIG!

LENA STORY

Lena gazed in the mirror- her fat rolls were looking fine today, all wubbery and rubbery, like a seal which had rolled around in a slick, scum-coated tidal pool full of rotting flotsam.

But there was still another step to go before her full glory could truly shine for the world- after all she had to go pose nude later, having gotten her latest payment from the bulimia treatment group which was secretly sponsoring her. She had to wax that shit and wax it good, so that her mottled skin would gleam like the shield of some ancient goddess- a goddess which, archaeologists assured her, was morbidly obese.

She giggled, and a sound like a sea lion in heat was emitted from her cheeks as she thought about how she was culturally appropriating the tactics of slave owners auctioning off other human beings- the naughtiness! How taboo! It really titillated her and she squirmed her sinful thighs together, squelching some wax into the creases and folds of her flesh.

She pulled out a picture of Donald Trump and rolled some marijuana up inside of it, sticking it in her rectum and smoking it up her intestines by tensing and relaxing her anal muscles. The munchies set in- good thing she had just received a special delivery from Trump Tower itself. "Damn you, Donald" she thought, as she smashed burgers and fries indiscriminately down her distended gullet, "I really want to be a vegetarian but your meat... your unholy meat... it's too much to resist!"

The cameras were ready. Like the irrelevant monstrosity she was, she threw on a robe, to be soon tossed aside, and proceeded to her destiny- all that greasy trickling down her mouth, all the sticky trickling down her legs... it was all Donalds doing.

ORANGE MAN BIG!

ALVIN STORY

Greasy burger drippings slowly made their way down the crenelated folds of Alvins chin, into his second chin, finally ending up on the ponderous third, strands of the stuff making their way in a slothful manner down to his cheap tie- it was a clip on, because his fingers were too obese for him to fashion a real one, although some days he privately confided that he wanted to fashion a noose so he could end his miserable existence. All the hamburgers in the world would not stave off the sense of dread he felt- after all, he was a district attorney in a very liberal area, and liberals were notably fickle- he was basically counting time before someone more radical than him forced him into retirement.

The burger was exhausted. He rubbed his many chins and plastered some of the greaseburger filth on his chest, feeling the warmth of the dead animal squeezings saturate his skin- oh what a joy! But it lasted only briefly. He was edging himself in his office chair, thinking about how great a whole heaping platter of meat would be.

The buzzer on his desk went off- a delivery had been made, but the sender hadn't identified themselves- a letter, and a bunch of small boxes which smelled like hot pickles, fat-fried spuds, and plenty of cow flesh. His sclerotic eyes opened wider than Epsteins piss hole during a toothpick party trick.

"Did the drug dog detect anything?" He said into the intercom.

"No." Came the simple reply.

"Any white powder that isn't related to donuts?"

"Negative."

ORANGE MAN BIG!

"Okay, send it up."

Within a minute the packages lay before him- five boxes and a note. His peepee was throbbing as much as his belly as he read it: "Dear Alvin. I know you're a hungry man, and we have so much extra food here. You've been trying to stuff me like a trophy but I only want to stuff you like a glutton. I know you're into that. By the way, send my regards to judge whats-his-name. Eat up my man, kangaroo courts should be stocked with kangaroo meat. Pretty tasty. Nothing on my burgers though. My burgers are the best. Always well done. No listeria. Your friend- 'Big D.'"

He marveled as he tore the boxes apart like a jaguar would crack the skull of a small monkey, practically shoving his muzzle into the feed inside. Like a pig finding a pile of discarded corn cobs on a beachside shipwreck, he flailed his tongue and mouth through the contents- burgers- a flat dozen of them- with fries, heaped high with condiments- there was ketchup, mayo, mustard, there was a milkshake. An entire pan of spicy fried chicken laid like tasty corpse pieces next to a platter of onion rings. Everything was perfect. Tears came from his eyes and sweat poured from his porcine flesh as he mashed the food around in his mouth, as though he had not eaten for a week- and he stopped edging, for the extra salt caused his blood pressure to rise, and his half stiff little weewee finally blossomed into a true mushroom. His pants were coated in slime, his shirt and suit in salty grease, his nipples protruding in an obscene manner as he rubbed onion rings on them, crying and pounding the table because of his sin.

Big D- his special secret friend- had his back, even though he was currently dragging him through politically motivated legal woes- and that was a touching thought. An hour later, as the calories wore off, he fell into a prediabetic slumber and spent the rest of his work day drooling on his desk like a fucking baby.

ORANGE MAN BIG!

JOHNNY STORY

Johnny was hungry. He was always hungry. Donald Trump had beaten him badly years ago because he couldn't stop eating- usually in a grotesque manner, stuffing his face with grinders, pizza, steak, or anything else he could find to stuff into his gullet.

Today was no exception- but the kitchen didn't have any of the good, greasy, salty stuff he really wanted, and he cried profusely, tears staining his cheap and ill-fitted suit as he slowly crammed saltine crackers into his mouth like a dwarf tossing coal into a furnace, morose, brooding, ruing the day.

A knock at the door almost made him choke on the dry, stale crackers, like Dubya at a pretzel eating contest. Who could it be? Through the window at the top of his door, he could just see a tuft of hair waving slightly in the breeze.

He waddled to the door and opened it- and there he was- in all his glory- the man who had humiliated him and made him have a half a dozen wet dreams over the years- it was Donald Trump, standing aloof, holding a gigantic platter, steam wafting from its sides as he made his way into the room, not bothering to ask if he could, and ignoring the sputtering Johnny as he set the platter down on the kitchen table.

"Nice place." Donald said, and Johnny felt his little weewee twinge slightly. "Not as nice as my place. Actually have dozens of them- did you know I can sleep anywhere I want to? One time I slept inside of a hollow tree, after I bought a forest and wanted to develop a golf course there. Golf is the best sport."

Johnny was silent; partly since he didn't know how to respond, but more because the steaming platter in front of him smelled awfully good.

ORANGE MAN BIG!

"I brought some wine too. Trump wine. We make it from the best grapes. American grapes."

The platter was soon companioned by a nice chardonnay. Johnny knew there must be fish or chicken in the platter and, without even saying a word, he grabbed the lid- burning his fingers a bit in the process- steam whirled its way out like a tornadic vortex, and the feast was revealed- a pile of fried fish, a huge pan of fries, and about a dozen different dipping sauces. He tore into the codfish and it was awfully good, and smeared the fries on his face, sopping the grease into his skin as Trump opened the wine. "Drink up my man, I have to go take a leak."

Hefting the fry pan in one arm and guzzling the wine like he was at a college party, Johnny attempted to furtively look through the bathroom door- which Donald had not closed- as he stuffed himself, beginning to feel tipsy. His member throbbed as he thought about catching just a glimpse of the mushroom in chief, but to no avail. The sound of Trumps piss slamming into the toilet bowl like Niagra Falls made his own penis blossom like Viagra Falls.

But after the flush, Donald was nowhere to be found once he finally got up the courage to check on him- still scarfing the food. The man had climbed through the bathroom window and left him all this food! He sniffed and licked the toilet bowl, then scraped off the piss and shit residue from it, smearing the paste on his food and moaning as he continued to eat, eventually passing out drunk on the bathroom floor in a pile of french fries. All the depraved perversion inside of him bubbled its way through drunken, strange dreams- dreams about frolicking hand and hand with his favorite feeder through a land where hamburgers and fried chicken grew on trees and all the fish in the sea were already cooked and came with tartar sauce.

ORANGE MAN BIG!

ERIC STORY

Eric shoveled down the last bowl of extra spicy canned baked beans and felt his tummy rumbling- it was show time. He bent over the desk and shoved his stomach into the edge, releasing a wispy cloud of fart gas which pooted out of his asshole with a sound like a trumpet. What a great feeling. He was out of beans though- he had worked his way through five cans already and was about to begin on his cauliflower and broccoli mix when his congressional office door swung open- there, in all his glory, was his arch nemesis, Donald Trump.

"Donald! You old crook! What the hell are you doing here at my sacred anal time?" Eric was livid, his greasy skin sweated profusely- perhaps the Don was here as part of an insurrection or something, but as Eric visually searched his hands for weapons, Don simply stood there, grinning like a crocodile in the doorway, and the only thing he was holding was a spray canister.

"I heard you were a man of special needs, Eric, so I figured I'd hire someone to give you the fist of fury, but I couldn't find anyone to do that so I brought the next best thing. Not as good as the things I own, I own lots of things, Eric, when you're rich, they let you."

Donald raised the sprayer and fired out a stream of slightly off-yellow mist at Eric, who immediately worried it was a nerve agent or something, and he dove under his desk, as Trump guffawed merrily, dancing around and rambling incoherently about the US border. A terrified Eric, pants still down around his ankles, could smell something horrendous... something wonderful.

It was then that he knew what was in Trumps' little spray bottle- it was bottled fart spray! He leaped up to vault over the desk, hoping to snatch the precious fluid, but his belt caught on the office chair and he tumbled smack down onto the desk, papers coming loose, rising up and falling through the air like so many leaves, as he scrambled to get his pants entirely off. He had to remove his shoes- sniffing them too. The smell of fine French cheeses filled his nostrils, making him obscenely turned on in the process.

Another shot of the ass gas hit him right in the face and he couldn't help any longer- humiliated with his ass bare for the entire world- and with several staffers outside gawking in at the window- where his ass sat shining and slightly dirty- available for anyone in the world to be disgusted at- he had an involuntary ejaculation on the desk, laying there, hobbled by his pants and strung to the office chair.

"Okay well, sorry Eric, glad you had a good time, but I have to go to a yuge rally in an hour or so. Gotta go make America great again and stuff, people like greatness and I like America. God bless us all." He carefully positioned the little spray bottle just out of reach, as Eric continued to claw his way forward, trying to grab it and savor the rich, nauseating scent of fart. He wished he had a Chinese envoy on hand to help him out- they were always very nice to him.

Trump left the room and closed the door behind him. Eric continued to writhe, coated in his own sperm and still pooting as he struggled for over ten minutes to extract himself, finally huffing the gassy smells out of a paper bag and getting literally high, becoming delirious before he finally went to go attend the next congressional vote- nobody noticed anything strange or different as he acted and smelled much as he always did.

THE END

Printed in Great Britain
by Amazon